Clarice Bean

My Uncle is a Hunkle

On Colour

NORMAL SERVICE WILL BE RESUMED AS SOON AS POSSIBLE

Lauren Child

My Uncle is a hunkle.

He says things like **Gotcha Baby**
and
Eat dirt ding bat.

He watches too many films.

He's a fireman so he wears special trousers. He's always rescuing people from tall toppling buildings which are going up in a cloud of smoke.

He can have you in a fireman's lift
before you can say

Uncle Ted put me down!

He says
he has had
plenty of close shaves
which is funny
because he has a beard.
Mum says me and
Uncle Ted get on
like a house on fire.

This book is for my
sister Rachel, who was
crazy about guinea pigs
and for my sister Jenny,
who preferred cars.

RACHEL

JENNY

♡ also for
my friend
Lindsay
Isobel
Hart

Thanks
to Olga
at the
guinea
pig
rescue
centre

ORCHARD BOOKS
First published in 2000 by Orchard Books
This edition published in 2009 by The Watts Publishing Group

10 9 8 7 6

Text and illustrations © Lauren Child 2000 and 2009
The moral rights of the author and illustrator have been asserted.

A CIP catalogue record for this book is
available from the British Library.

ISBN 978 1 40830 006 0

Printed in China

FSC
www.fsc.org
MIX
Paper from
responsible sources
FSC® C104740

Orchard Books
An imprint of Hachette Children's Group
Part of The Watts Publishing Group Limited

Carmelite House, 50 Victoria Embankment
London EC4Y 0DZ

An Hachette UK company.
www.hachette.co.uk

www.hachettechildrens.co.uk

This book
has been printed
on paper made
from sustainable
forest timber.

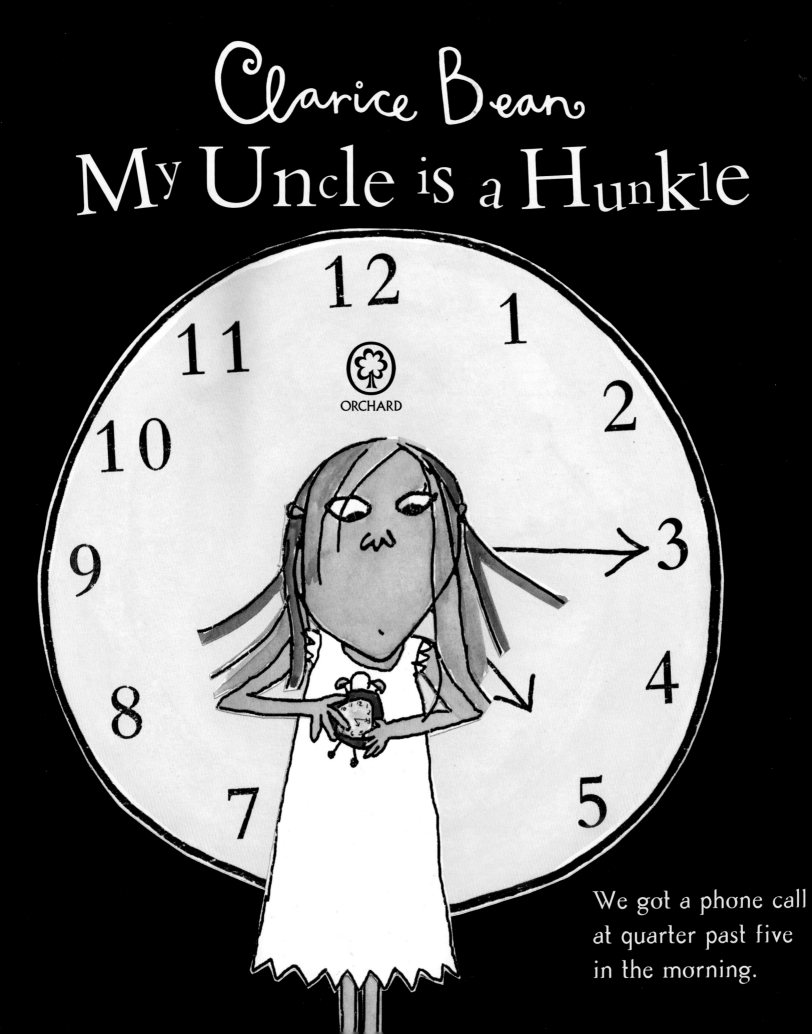

Clarice Bean
My Uncle is a Hunkle

We got a phone call
at quarter past five
in the morning.

It turned out Uncle Ernie *slipped* on a doughnut getting out of his squad car.

He's a policeman in New York City so he's used to life's ups and *downs.*

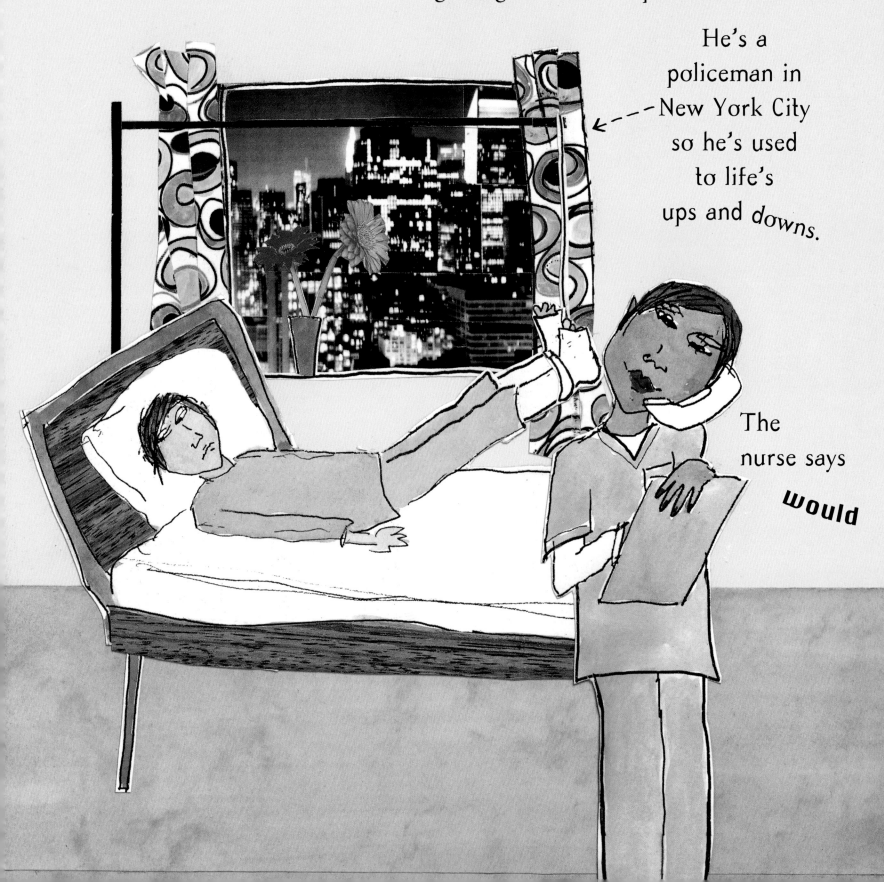

The nurse says **would**

Someone will have to babysit because
Dad is also about to go away on Important Business.

Marcie (my big sister) says,
**I would rather look after newts
from Neptune than
be left with Clarice Bean** (me)
and Minal Cricket
(my little brother).

Kurt
(my big brother)
says,
**Don't look at me, I'm going
to my room and probably
won't be down for supper.**

Minal says,
What
about
Grandad?

Grandad says,
I haven't had
a doughnut
since I was
a boy.

Mum rings round all her friends for a babysitter.
Then she rings round all her
friends' friends
but everybody says
they are busy.

Dad says,
Who can
blame them?

I'll be with you
in two shakes,
Bernard.

I say,
How about
Uncle
Ted?

Mum goes a bit pale.

Uncle Ted is Mum's younger brother.

When Uncle Ted fancies a break from fire fighting
and cats up trees he comes round to our house.
Whenever he's
around it gets really noisy.

Get off your horse
and drink your milk.

Uncle Ted and I love to watch westerns on the edge of our seats
with a plate of egg and beans
perched on our laps.

Uncle Ted is teaching me cowboy techniques.
Last week he lassoed the lamp.

Mum said,
I'd rather have everything in one piece
thank you very much.

Uncle Ted looked sheepish.
I lassoed my brother.
He wasn't too happy either.

So you can see why Mum is nervous about leaving Uncle Ted in charge but it turns out she can't be so choosy. Mum gives Uncle Ted some **very** strict instructions.

1. NO BREAKAGES

2. NO LASSOING

3. DON'T DRIVE MRS STAMPNEY AT NUMBER 9 DOO-LALLY

4. MAKE SURE KURT SEES THE DAYLIGHT AT LEAST ONCE EVERY 24 HOURS

6. KEEP AN EYE ON GRANDAD HE TENDS TO WANDER OFF

5. DON'T LET MARCIE TAKE THE PHONE INTO HER BEDROOM

chat chat chat chat chat chat chat chat chat

Uncle Ted says,

**Yes Maam.
I hear you
loud and clear.**

Everything goes **really well** for the first two days.

Nobody is arguing and we are like one of those families on your television who always say things like

please

and

thank you

and

sorry . . .

...and they let people share their things without grumbling.

Kurt even sits in the garden and almost nearly gets a tan. He never normally goes outside, he says it's too bright.

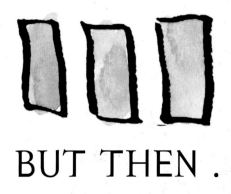

BUT THEN . . .

Minal ruins everything
by getting Albert out of his hutch without asking.
I am the one looking after him for the holidays.
(Albert is the school guinea pig so it's a VERY
RESPONSIBLE
JOB.)

Albert

Albert makes

To take my mind
off the worry of
losing a guinea pig
we all go outside
    and play football.
And it works because

Uncle Ted kicks the ball so hard that it knocks Minal out.

We have to
drive
to the
e
m
e
r
g
e
n
c
y

*Hang
on
to
your
trousers.*

r
o
o
m
at
50
miles
an hour
at least!

Minal is fine
but they give him an X-ray
and a little carton of orange juice.

Minal loves it
because he can
show off and lie
under a blanket
whimpering.

I say he should
have stitches but
unfortunately the
nurse doesn't agree.

When we get home we find Grandad is missing.
Uncle Ted phones round all the neighbours
and is about to dial 999 when
Mrs Stampney at Number 9
calls to say she has found Grandad
sitting
in
her
sitting room.

Watching the racing.

She's quite grumpy about it.

Uncle Ted says,

How in tarnation did you end up here?

Grandad says,
    All the houses look the same,
it's **a job** to tell them **apart without my glasses.**

    But I know it's really because
Mrs Stampney's got a bigger television set than us
            and it's got a remote control.

I'm still worried to pieces about Albert so I go into the garden to see if he has come back to his hutch.

I had put a carrot there
to tempt him back
but
it is still unnibbled.

The next thing I know,
Robert Granger,
the boy next door,

pops over

the wall.

He says,
Do you want to stroke **my guinea pig?**

I say, That's not
your
guinea pig that's Albert.

He says,
It's not Albert
she's Belinda.

I say,
You better give him back
Robert Granger
that's School Property
and you will be
in
big trouble
with the Police.

Robert Granger is so nervous
he lets Albert
wriggle
out of his hands.

Albert is
s c u t t l i n g
through
the house

We are
madly
c h a s i n g
the
loose
guinea pig who
is
c h a r g i n g
through the
railings.

Uncle Ted shouts,
After him.

and
out
of
the
front
door.

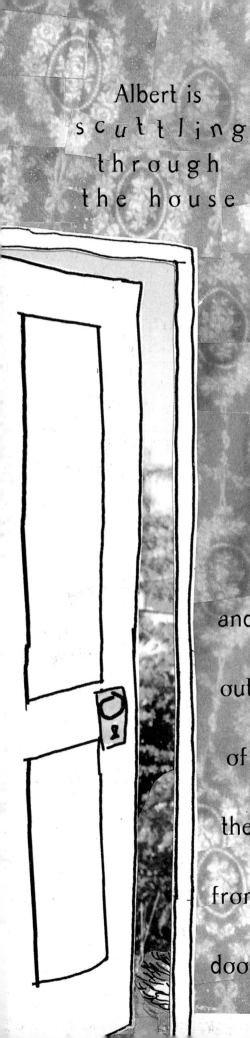

Minal squeezes past him and gets wedged like a giant squeaking tomato.
I say,
Lucky you are here Uncle Ted because you will have him rescued in next to no time.

(Rescuing people from railings is normal for Uncle Ted and he doesn't look a bit bothered.)

Uncle Ted says,
Hang in there Buddy,

and he shoots off to call his friends at the fire station. But it takes him ages to find the phone.

chat
chat
chat
chat
. . . so anyway,
I said . . .
chat   chat
chat
. . . and then guess
what he said . . .

chat

chat
chat
chat
chat

In the meantime,
Mum arrives back from the airport.
She delves straight in her bag
for her new bottle of bubble bath
and rubs it on Minal's head.
She squidges him out in almost
less than two
minutes.

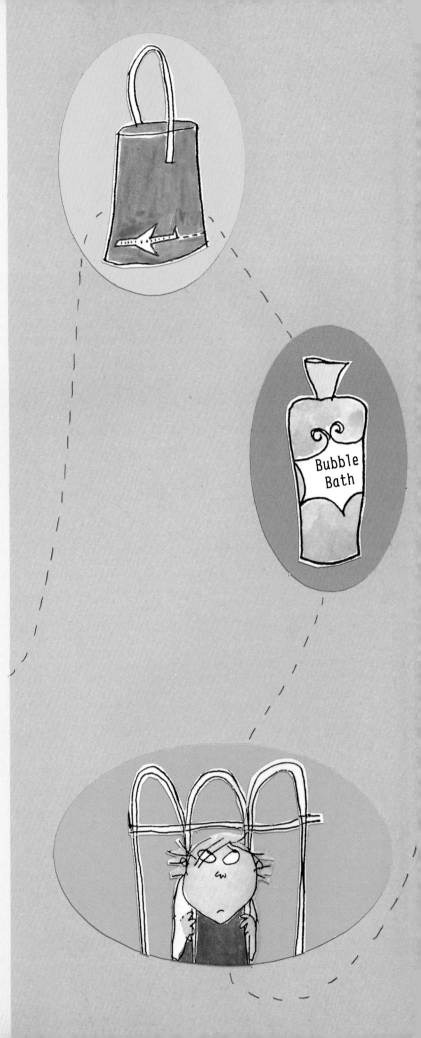

She says, I wouldn't mind a quiet cup of tea in the garden.

But then guess what happens?

Nearly all the whole
fire brigade turns up.
Mum doesn't
even look one bit
surprised.
She just looks at
Uncle Ted.

Minal,
already rescued

It turns out Uncle Ernie is feeling quite chirpy now but he doesn't think he will ever be able to look at a doughnut again.

He says,
Mine's a
**double
cheeseburger**
with **fries** and a
**banana
milkshake** to go.